HISTORY OF A DEAD MAN

A SACRED KNIGHT TALE

DAWN BLAIR

MORNING SKY STUDIOS

BOOKS BY DAWN BLAIR:

Sacred Knight

Quest for the Three Books

Manifest the Magic

To Birth a Destiny

History of a Dead Man (companion novella)

Prince of the Ruined Land

The Loki Adventures

1-800-Mischief

For Sale, Call Loki

For A Good Time, Call Loki

For More Information, Call Loki

For More Mischief, Call Loki

1-800-CallLoki (Omnibus of novellas 1-5)

1-800-IceBaby (coming soon)

Wells of the Onesong

Fractured Echo

Fall's Confession

The Doorway Prince

Stardust

Mystery of the Stardust Monk

Ninjas

By the Numbers

Space Ninjas Aren't Real

Other stories

The Last Ant

Broken Smiles

Oxygen

I'm With Cupid

Let's Make a Deal

Nonfiction

The Write Edit

Children's Picture Books

Eggs at Play

AUTHOR'S NOTE

This novella is part of the Sacred Knight series and is meant to be read between the third and fourth books to fill in a gap there. But don't panic!

If you haven't read the series, this story will hopefully give you an overview but it does have a couple spoilers. Still, reading this then going back to the series with the knowledge gained here might actually enhance your reading experience and bring on the suspense!

Just be warned that I don't stop to explain a whole lot; I do expect that readers have read the first three books (series to date: *Quest for the Three Books, Manifest the Magic, To Birth a Destiny*). But don't worry if this is your first venture into the Sacred Knight world. Consider it a sample. I hope it will inspire you to read the rest when you're done here.

For those familiar with the series, I've included a section called The Story Behind the Tale to give you information on why you are getting this interlude as told from Annae's point of view. It's not important to read it if you just want to jump to the story, but if you are interested in seeing how an author fashions a story (and some of the "insanity" we go through in telling our stories) then you'll find it interesting.

THE STORY BEHIND THE TALE

For two decades now, I've been writing about the lives of Steigan and Saint Steigan.

I have countless drafts of my first attempts at The Three Books. I wrote a lot. I stored a lot on paper, floppy disc, and hard drive space. At times I wanted to give up. I cried on the shoulder of frustration as this story became mammoth and threatened to overwhelm me. But great projects in our life should both scare and inspire us. How would I write this book, this series, so that it retained the complexity of the story but carried the simplicity I wanted in the words?

The answer to that was just to keep writing. Lots! I hope you get the picture here. I had a jumble of scenes in my head and sometimes they made sense and at other times they didn't. The story even changed genres a couple of times, which I've discussed on my various blogs.

Somewhere along the way, I discovered that I had several years that St. Steigan never talked about. I'm sure it happened when I was still exploring the story, but I don't recall when exactly I realized that St. Steigan had shut me out of forty to fifty years of his life. I was so use to him letting me be privy to his innermost thoughts that it took a while for me to realize that something had to have happened during the time that he closed off and would only say, "I raised Annae." Mind you, when I first saw the child about four years old in my head I really believed Annae to be Steigan's daughter with Keteria. I was good with that being his answer and I didn't question it further.

Then in one draft I had Steigan find St. Steigan's journal leaving him clues as to the whereabouts of three hidden books Steigan was searching for, I realized these missing years were more important than previously imagined. I had to know why these journals were written. I went to St. Steigan again determined to do an author/character interview to find out. Instead, I ended up begging him for months for information and him responding with so much pain that I could no longer bear it. I now thought of the period Steigan wouldn't talk about as his missing years. If he didn't want to tell me, so be it.

Another aspect of the story I was starting to feel neglected was the celebrations of this world. When I went to Steigan to ask him about holidays and ceremonies, he shrugged and told me it was just another day for him. I honestly had to do an interview with Steigan's friend, Martias, in order to get details about their daily lives and special days. Steigan had such a limited view of the world; he was in survivor mode and when I was in Steigan's head I didn't realize how bleak his life felt. There is very little detail in The Three Books because it is a reflection of how Steigan viewed his every day.

Now that I had a grip of the story and started to get serious about writing The Three Books, I prepared an outline across the entire series. I realized these journals St. Steigan had written were important and I'd have to know more about the missing years.

"I'll tell you," a little girl's voice said. "Daddy. The simple word had the power to bring tears to his eyes."

I grabbed a notebook and started writing. "Why?" I asked.

She told me her story. We spent two weeks together, me writing as fast as I could put it on paper. I revised and added to as I entered it all into my computer. Then I put it aside. I had what I needed. The greatest tragedy in St. Steigan's life had been revealed. While she told me the events St. Steigan wouldn't talk about, I felt his pain. I now knew why he would never speak about what had happened.

As I got to writing Manifest the Magic and To Birth a Destiny, my series outline went out the window and I was writing completely fresh material. I took the time to draft them as one long story, which I then split into two. I knew what events had to happen to get St. Steigan where I needed him, since Annae had already told me. I dug out her story once more and it became paramount in me getting the incidents in place.

The original tale that Annae told me several years before wasn't perfect. There were a few occurrences out of order. I wanted to polish the story and get it in line with the third book before I could move onto writing the fourth in the series. I'm glad I did. When I did the outline of the series, I hadn't taken into account the anguish caused by St. Steigan's missing years. I hadn't expected my own rollercoaster of emotions with Steigan back in the timeline from The Three Books. How could Steigan live with this knowledge?

I'm still working on that part and don't know the answer yet.

What started off as backstory information I wanted to know has grown into a tale of its own. If you don't believe me, check out the prologue in the second book, Manifest the Magic. This is the very story that Annae petitioned the Council of Lords to give her funds for. In The Three Books,

Aeribela mentions a book written by Annae, one that she believes hers to be the only copy. This novella is the account that Aeribela had read.

I am now happy to share with you the story of Annae's life: St. Steigan's missing years. Enjoy!

HISTORY OF A DEAD MAN

I sat on my father's lap in the darkened room, his warm arms around me. His heart pounded and an occasional shudder ripped through him. I felt like sobbing and I wondered if he did too. Even at ten cycles old, I knew this new situation to be wrong.

Only moments before, a strange man had stumbled into the house, the door slamming behind him. Dirt splattered the stranger's green shirt and the lacings hung loose as if he'd been too hung over from the previous night to do them up correctly earlier that morning.

"Come here, Annae," I heard my father's deep voice call softly. It felt like a strong undertow current, safe and familiar, compared to the chaotic, cresting waves on the surface.

I left my seat at the square, wooden table and dashed for the room which served as my father's library. As I skirted around the stranger, I half expected him to reach for me, but his dark, glassy eyes never left my mother as she ran her fingers through his disheveled hair. The scent of smoke and ale stirred in the air as they laughed and moved through the kitchen, heading deeper into the house, arms grabbing and tangling each other as if drowning and gasping for life.

Roused by the commotion, my dad had hobbled to the doorway and stared venomously at the embracing couple. He scooped me up in his arms and took me into the secluded room, closing the door behind us. His walking cane thumped hard against the floor as he went around the room and blew out all the candles as if pretending we weren't even there. Then he sat down on the floor against the wall with me on his lap.

A resounding thump followed trilling laughter. I glanced toward the door, wondering if they were coming into the library too. "Da?" I asked fearfully. Dad placed one hand on my head, covering my ear so the only sound I heard was his heartbeat. Was he struggling to keep me from hearing the stranger?

As the ticks deepened, he began to tap his head against the wall behind him as if he could bang out the frustration he felt. I tried to look up at him, wondering if his expression would give me an explanation for what was going on, but I couldn't see him in the dark.

At last, he stood up, awkwardly bracing himself with the cane while holding me and carried me outside to the forge house. I glanced around, awed by the blacksmithing tools and creations he had in here. Normally, I wasn't allowed inside, but the arrival of the stranger with my mother granted me an exception, though I wasn't quite sure why. Pliers, hammers, pinchers all arranged neatly on the wall, tables set with different size anvils, nails, horseshoes, chain-mail, plate armor, swords, arrow tips.

Setting his cane against the wall, Dad opened a cupboard and pulled out a cloth sack. Inside the sack, wrapped again in more cloth, he took out a loaf of bread and handed a chunk of it to me. "Sit and eat up," he said, then he set to work. His gait took on a more pronounced limp as he walked around unaided. Tonight, I could tell, his leg bothered him more than usual and he'd probably looked forward to spending the evening writing at his desk as he did most nights after supper. Instead, he'd been driven out here. He removed his vest, hung it from a hook on the door, and put on a leather apron which had been hanging from another peg.

The hot, metallic odor of blacksmithing stung the inside of my nose and I could barely bring myself to eat, but I did anyway as I watched my father work. His tunic grew damp with sweat as he worked over the forge and pounded away at softened metal. His short black hair was soon plastered to his head.

With the heat and my belly filled with bread, I felt my eyes grow heavy. Rhythmic tapping urged me to sleep. I wanted to stay awake, to watch my father work, to know when the man would leave our house, to know why he was there, but all my curiosities fell away like sparks blown from the bellows when Dad would stoke the forge's fire and more warmth surrounded me.

I woke for but a moment when Dad sat down beside me and pulled me against him. I felt him slide the rolled up vest beneath my head, picking away a piece of straw stuck to my cheek.

"Little Annae, I'm so sorry," Dad whispered into my hair before he breathed in deeply. "It should have been me."

I woke before Dad the next morning, though my stirring roused him. He helped me to my feet, then straightened my hair with his fingers, pulling out more straw, and adjusted my clothes so they didn't look like I'd been sleeping all night in them though I had. He licked his thumb to wipe a smudge from my face and gave me a reassuring smile as if to say it would be all right. I believed him.

I didn't want the strange man to still be in the house.

Dad took my hand and guided me along the cobblestone walkway to the door. The morning chill vanished as warmth from the fires of the kitchen hearth greeted us along with the scent of baking bread. It suddenly felt like a regular day. The normal moment almost erased the abnormality of the night. We came into the kitchen where Mother was making breakfast. She turned at our arrival and wiped the back of her wrists hurriedly over her cheeks. Rushing to put down the knife she'd been holding, she rubbed her hands inside her apron, then dried her red eyes once more. She'd been crying for a while.

Dad released my hand as my mother dashed over and hugged me.

"I thought you might have taken her away forever," Mom said, her hands flat against my back, pressing me closer to her.

"If you want to act like a dog, keep it out of the house and away from Annae." He started to step by her, but hesitated. "I will not be put through that again." He continued on to the washroom.

How could my mother and father have come to this? I knew we were different from other families. I'd seen the way my friend's parents acted together and wondered why mine didn't do the same, but I'd been too young to understand why mine slept in separate rooms. It was our little secret which we hid from the world behind well-chosen lies.

To the outside world, we seemed like the perfect family. A mother and father swinging their young daughter between them, all of us smiling and laughing as we headed to Cliff Park in Dubinshire for the annual Springsday Festival, the annual celebration kicking off our holiday season. Dad would participate in the sword challenge. I loved watching the young boys take on my father; none of them could ever land a blow unless he let them. Which he did; he always let the boys win. Lord Freygorio, ruler of Dubinshire, would jest about another defeat and tease my father about losing his edge, but Dad and I knew the truth: he was a great dominus and had fought in many battles for the Temple, defending the Goddess from naysayers. It's how his leg had gotten injured and his face scarred.

My mother and I were so proud of him. Or I thought we were.

Dad made sure I had the best schooling, lining me up to become a Temple historian. It suited my intellect and penmanship, he had once told me. Little did I know that I had the biggest piece of history right in front of me.

One evening when I was about thirteen cycles old or so, Dad and I were in his library after supper, as was our usual custom. I had my lessons spread out on the table before me. Dad sat at the desk nearby, two books open before him as he copied text from one into the other. I couldn't read the beautiful scrolling writing, but I couldn't stop watching how it flowed effortlessly from his quill.

He paused to ink the tip and saw me staring at him. "What did you learn today in your classes?" he asked with a sad smile.

"Your friend, Sapere Hyrin, came in today and spoke about the ethics of history," I replied.

He went back to his writing. "So what did he say about the ethics of history?"

"He said that it meant we, as historians, had a job to record events like they really happened and not let our emotions cloud it. We have to be truthful and unbiased in our chronicles. He said we shouldn't be influenced by what others would have us record."

Dad frowned at the page he was working on. "What if that endangers the lives of those around you?"

"I didn't think to ask that. But why would the truth endanger people?"

"Did he care to give you any examples?"

"He spoke about Saint Steigan and how he was a dominus who first transformed the Temple at Lilinar, then nearly destroyed it. Sapere Hyrin said that period of time became known as The Breaking and the Reunification in Lilinar, which is now dubbed New Lilinar to fully mark that devastating era as concluded."

Dad put his quill down and covered his face with his hands.

A terrible thought hit me. "Were you there? Did you fight against Saint Steigan?"

Tears caught in the candle's light highlighted the bitter pain across his face. "The Temple was in flames, walls crumbled, there was smoke everywhere. The Breaking was a terrible time to be in Lilinar. Saint Steigan put you and your mom in a wagon and got you out."

"Why don't you tell her the truth?" Mom's small voice asked from the doorway where she'd been listening.

Dad slammed his hands on the desk as he stood. "Have you been conspiring with Sapere Hyrin now? You will not destroy this family!" He grabbed up his cane and started toward her. I wondered if he would strike her with it. "I have worked too hard to let you break it up," he shouted at her.

Mom fled and shortly the house door slammed behind her. She was gone for the evening. Dad's shoulders slumped forward and he stood there for a moment before turning back toward me. I wondered if I might get the truth, whatever it was that Dad was hiding from me. Instead, he limped over to the table and put his hands over mine. He looked like he was about to say something, then patted my hand. "'Tis time to get ready for bed. Go on."

I knew now that Sapere Hyrin had been telling me that

history contained lies because some things were too terrible to drag into the light even within families. I also had been given a mystery within my own house. What did my parents know that they were trying so hard to keep from me?

The next day, Dad walked with me to school as was customary, but after he sent me off, I watched him continue on toward the Dubinshire Castle. I figured he was going to the Temple inside the castle to meet with Hyrin and I followed secretly behind him. I'd been to visit Hyrin enough times with my Dad that I knew exactly where I'd find them. With it being a beautiful fall day, I found the window open and heard the men speaking within.

"I assure you, Searn," Hyrin said, "it was not my intention to give away Saint Steigan's secrets. I just feel it might help to ease current tensions if we let it be known why he destroyed the Cauldron of Life."

"Magic is gone from the world in its entirety. Even having the waters from the Cauldron would not restore it either to the maeges or to children currently coming into the world. Saint Steigan is dead and his deeds are done. If that makes nations hate him, so be it. That hatred will fade as people move on. But those loyal to Saint Steigan must keep that devotion in their hearts and not try to give it away to salve the wounds of individuals who only want magic to return. A purchase of poorly given faith will never last."

I covered my mouth with my hands to keep from laughing. Not only did my father know St. Steigan, but they had been on the same side.

"Am I supposed to just keep quiet in my loyalty to Saint Steigan?" Hyrin asked.

"Walk the line, Sapere. The legacy Saint Steigan left for the Temple should not be forgotten, just recorded as history's victors would have it written."

"No real truth and no real lies? Hearsay then?"

"Hearsay," my father confirmed. "Until the day Saint Steigan rises again."

That ended their conversation, but inspired me to learn all I could about the notorious saint and betrayer of the Temple at Lilinar. Was there more to this man than the legacy he left behind? How did a new religion grow from words he spoke? How could he betray the very religion he created to the point of terrorizing them and murdering a Holy Sapere?

I'd had every intention of starting with my mother, who seemed to know as much as Dad did. I wondered if she would tell me the truth, if she disagreed with my father that much, I knew my chances were good.

But I returned home from classes that day to find my mother sick. She barely managed to cook dinner for us that night and went to bed before we sat down to eat. Dad told me she'd probably be fine by the next morning, but as a new day came, I found her in worse condition.

For nearly a fortnight, she was sick in the morning, then recovered some as the day progressed. The fact that she would not eat finally forced Dad to seek help for her. A woman came and took my mother aside into her room for a while. When the women emerged, Mom announced that she was going to have another baby.

"Da, are you happy?" I asked, thinking I would soon have a brother or a sister. Maybe now we could be a real family.

A strange look passed between my parents. Dad forced a smile. "I hope it brings your mother happiness. Then I will be content." He patted my shoulder and hugged my mother before going into his library and closing the door behind him.

As the months of the pregnancy progressed, my dad accepted congratulations from everyone who offered it. But when we were at home together, Dad avoided my mother.

When the midwife arrived to help the baby into the world, Dad left the house and went to the tavern. The man who'd come home with my mother on that night many cycles ago returned later with him. When the baby cried, Dad stayed with me while the man went into visit Mother and baby. 'Tis a boy, I was told. A brother. Someone Dad could teach to swordfight; he'd like that, wouldn't he? Of course he would.

The baby didn't make it through a fortnight.

I woke to a terrifying scream and ran down the hallway to my mother's room. Standing in the doorway, I listened to her horrid tears as she sobbed over the cradle, a little wood and iron rocker that Dad had made. It took a while for Dad to pull her away from the little body and when he did, she pummeled him with her fists.

"You did this! You smothered him last night, didn't you?"

At first, he took the beating until she started to swing as his scarred face, then he grabbed her hands and held her away from him. "I've taken away someone you loved once. I'd never take away your happiness again."

When she collapsed at his feet, he bent down to hug her. "The Goddess fell in love with his beauty and wanted to be surrounded by his light. He walks with Her now, and Searn."

Why had Dad spoken his own name as though he were dead?

Dad wrapped the little body in its blankets and left the house. He returned much later that day, his body sagged with weariness. He looked at Mother as though pleading with her not to fight with him anymore. "Sapere Hyrin will conduct the ceremony at nightfall. Holy Sapere Kelan said he would bestow a Crossing Blessing."

"You will be named as Crossing Father instead of Nikael?"

"Everyone already believes he's mine. No sense in letting them know otherwise."

She nodded her head and started to ask something, but held back. Dad noticed this and said, "Nikael will stand as Guardian in Second. It's already arranged."

"You've spoken to him?"

"I've never seen him more sober."

Mother raised her hands to her mouth as her eyes brimmed with tears. Dad hugged her and let her cry against him.

That night, my half-brother was burned on a pier near the cliffs. Dad stood a splendid sight in his full armor. Nikael, a sailor by trade, had borrowed a sword from Dad so they could walk in saluted fashion on either side of the pier before the fire was lit, with their swords crossed above the body. Mom leaned against the baker's wife for comfort and I felt suddenly discounted. The whole ceremony felt wrong and stiff and I wanted to shout for someone to explain all the things I'd heard and felt.

For the week afterwards, people brought food to the house every evening. Dad accepted it graciously, then left it on the table for us and went out to the forge. He'd pound metal until his leg hurt him so much, he came hobbling back in on his cane. Without it, he wouldn't have been able to walk at all. He'd crutch his way into his room and shut the door. Come morning, he'd be awake before anyone else and have breakfast made for me before taking me to class. Usually, he'd try to walk part of the way without the cane, but during that week he used the cane with every step.

"Teach me how to sword-fight like you do the boys," I said one day, hoping I could create some sort of reconciliation in our family, anything to soothe my father's pain. And if mother saw us, maybe our fun and laughter would make her smile again.

He rustled my hair with his big hand. "A girl should never have to fight."

"But the Goddess carries a sword and She always fights for what is right, like you do. Please, Da."

"I don't think your mother would approve."

Something about his tone and the way he said 'your mother' made me feel separated from him, and Mom apart from him as well. Why did he want distance between us? Weren't we family?

We made a stop on the way home from class that afternoon, so Dad could pick up a package wrapped in cloth.

That night after supper and I'd been sent to get ready for bed, Dad came in from the forge and handed the package to Mom. From the shadows of the hallway, I watched them in the kitchen. Mom looked questioningly at the package for a moment before she reached shaking hands out to pull the ribbon and unfolded the cloth.

Inside was a Memory Plaque with a clipping of my brother's red baby hair pressed between two pieces of glass and delicate wrought iron interlocking hearts scrolling together in a frame. Trembling fingers covered her lips. "You do care, don't you?"

He pulled a table chair up beside her and sat down. "I've always cared." He took her hands. "I'm sorry if you thought I didn't. Searn was my best friend and my only family. I just never thought of you as anything more than my cousin's wife. But I've always cared for you and I will give you anything within my power to give."

"Everything but your heart."

"Cen, you're confusing me for Searn. I'm not him. And my heart belongs to another."

I couldn't believe what I was hearing. Everyone called my father Searn, but here he was saying he wasn't Searn. How could that be? If he wasn't my father, who was he and why was he pretending?

"I know you're not Searn, and the woman you love is dead. Can't you let go so we can have a normal life together, give Annae the family she deserves?"

"I didn't come here to have a normal life. Don't you think I'd love to have a wife and family? But it's not why I'm here. I have my mission."

"Don't we all?"

"Some more than others. I'm a Dominari."

I'd never heard the title, Dominari, before. What exactly did it mean? How did it differ from a dominus?

"One who's supposed to be dead," my mother continued. "Why not enjoy a normal life now?"

"Because I have more to do. I can't have a normal life yet. I'm not done."

"You're crippled. Your fighting days are over. What help do you think you can possibly provide now?

"The books are my mission now. I have to write them. I have to make sure the future has what it needs."

"So I'll also be sacrificed for the mission?"

Dad ran his hands over his face in frustration. He took a deep breath, trying to calm himself before he spoke. "I wish it were different, but there's so much to prepare. It's on my shoulders and only I can fix what's going to come. You're free to make yourself happy. Find what you need where you need it, but don't assume that I don't care about you and Annae."

Mom still didn't look happy, but she picked up the Memory Plaque and held it close to her. "Annae is probably waiting for you to tuck her in."

I jumped to my feet and raced barefoot down the hall to my room, my heart racing with fear that I'd be caught eavesdropping on their moment, but when I looked back Dad had barely managed to get to his feet and start toward the hallway. I dove under the covers and waited for him to come in, pretending I hadn't heard their exchange.

The Memory Plaque hung in my mother's room until the day she passed through the veil to the afterlife.

I'd hoped that evening would end the strange distance between all of us, but it didn't and I had yet to discover how bad it would become between my parents. Mom continued going out nearly every night and would return laughing, singing, and carrying on so loudly it would rouse me from sleep. Quite often she had a new bobble of jewelry which she'd show me in the morning like it was a prize she'd won.

Meanwhile, Dad helped me with my studies after she'd leave. I'd wished for a break to research about a Dominari on my own, but my curriculums already took so much time and were getting harder for me. Dad had such a knack for teaching the lessons so I wouldn't forget them, but sometimes his words were spoken wrong in such a way it was like he'd memorized them incorrectly. It irritated him, I could tell, but he dove back into the material as though trying hard to relearn them himself. Still, his instructions and enthusiasm made me take to my lessons with passion.

These were quiet times between us, easy and stress-free. I cherished the moment Mom would leave and we'd retire to the library at sundown. I'd work on my studies and Dad would continue writing his texts.

One evening, I gathered up my pages to take over to my father and came to stand at his side while he wrote. The words were foreign but elegant. I never knew just what it was he worked on, had never thought to ask until that moment. It was just something that had always been, but now I knew this was part of a personal mission. "What does it say?"

Dad looked up at me, then turned in his chair to face me.

"The land where I come from has forgotten the words of the Goddess. I want to make sure they know the truth."

"Are you not from Dubinshire then?" I asked.

"No. 'Tis very far from here and you would not recognize it." He tapped the pages I held in my hands. "What question do you have now on your lessons?"

As soon as I finished, I was sent to bed and this was how our lives progressed for too short of a time.

Dad's leg worsened. He could no longer stand at the forge to do his blacksmithing for as long as he once had. I'd heard him tell Mom that Lord Freygorio had given him a position to train the youngest of the initiates at the Temple. He had to sit down to instruct now, but I still loved watching him on his stool as he instructed. I'd then find my own stick and mimic the moves he'd been teaching. I envied the boys, getting to sit at my father's feet and learn from him. When we were together, it was history and penmanship, never swords.

Mom, on the other hand, played while she left me with more of the chores to do. Her nights out got later and later and often she wasn't even awake in the morning when Dad took me to the Temple for my lessons. In the afternoons when we were all home together, very few words were spoken between us. Usually, it was my mother yelling about something while Dad replied in low tones. Once Mom left for the evening, tension in the house lifted. But on the nights she didn't leave, Dad stayed out of whatever room she was in.

All this time, Dad provided for us. Our clothes were fine cloth, maybe not quite the best material, but better than most people had. We always had enough food on the table, a lot of it being fresh from the garden he and Mom tended; it was one of the few things they did together where they didn't argue, mostly because outdoors they could be seen by neighbors and they seemed to have an unspoken agreement to never argue in public. Evenings in the garden during the summer were a peaceful time because they wouldn't fight and actually spoke to each other in normal tones. Until she got ready for her night on the town. She'd flaunt herself in front of Dad, and even later admitted she did. Unfortunately, she fought a battle she'd already lost.

In the routine of our lives, I nearly forgot about St. Steigan, Dominari, and that this man who was raising me wasn't my father.

On my seventeenth birthday, I had my Independence Blessing at the Temple. Dad bought me a fine white gown with silver thread woven into the fabric. I watched it sparkle in the sunlight as the open carriage drove me to the Temple. Somehow, Dad acquired two unicorns from the forest to pull the carriage. At first, the driver had refused to hitch the unicorns, but Dad convinced him the unicorns were happy to do this and the animals knew it was only temporary.

"After all this time, you're going to blow your cover," Mom whispered as she gazed at the unicorns.

Dad shrugged. "Only the best for your little girl."

Upon arriving at the Temple, fresh, yellow strickleberry flower petals were scattered over the floor. A love of strickleberries was something Dad and I shared and he'd taken me often into the woods to gather the berries, many times eating a quarter of what we had gathered so we returned home with purple lips as evidence of our transgression. Outfitted in his armor, he walked me slowly up the aisle to the podium without his cane.

"Let me get your cane, Da," I protested as he nearly fell. I knew I wouldn't be strong enough to catch him and keep him up.

"A dominus shows no weakness," he whispered sharply back at me. Then he tried to soften it with a smile, but I knew his pride had taken offense.

Somehow, I made it to the altar, Dad made it to his seat, and the ceremony continued.

Once we were home, I went to change. I came back in time to hear my mother say, "It would have been a great day for Searn to see."

"This is her day. Don't ruin it."

"Aye, her day. A day when she should have had both of her parents with her. I'm going to tell her today."

"Fine. My duty to you and her are fulfilled."

Dad stormed into the library and slammed the door behind him. A moment later, I heard a crash. I ran out of the hallway into the kitchen. Mom looked at me with the same expression of shock and worry I was certain I had my face. We were both afraid that his leg had given out on him after being on it all day without his cane. But when we opened the door to the library, we found Dad slumped over the table where we had always done my lessons. He pounded his fists on the wood as he cried like I'd never seen anyone do before. Mom stopped me from entering the room. Rage took him as he crossed the small distance to his desk and he swept his arm over the surface sending books and papers flying. An inkwell toppled on the floor, splattering black droplets all over the wood, desk, and papers. He screamed and stumbled backwards, slumping awkwardly to the floor where he sat with his forehead on his knee and his arms flung over his head against the same wall where he'd once held me.

He still didn't know we were behind him. "Da...?" I asked, feeling my stomach tighten.

Tears spilled down over his scarred face now wrinkled with terrible despair. I'd never seen so much pain. Not even anger, just pain.

"Daddy?" I asked again as fear twisted through me.

"Aren't you going to tell her? Tell her about my lies?" Dad

asked roughly, his voice sounding like he'd swallowed hot coals.

I turned to Mom, waiting to know what could possibly be so catastrophic.

"'Tis time you knew." Mom's eyes flooded with tears even as they sharpened with vindictiveness. She put her hand on my shoulder. But her lips tightened; she couldn't bring herself to say it.

"He's not my father, is he?" I had to be the one to say the words. I had to ask the question, even though I already knew the truth. In doing so, I resented my mother's weakness.

"No," Mom answered. "He was a friend of your father's and your father died saving his life."

So there it was. The words I was so afraid to hear were real. How many times had I suspected it was true? My mother's anger suddenly made sense; my childhood had been built on a lie she'd been forced to live with this man who felt obligated to take care of us.

"He's wishing it was your dad here to see you today, not him. He robbed Searn of seeing every special event in your life," Mom said. All the bitterness in her words became my own.

"Why has he been living as Searn Bytherhourn? Who is he really?" I asked.

"No one must know who he really is, except those who knew him before."

"Before what?" I asked. I had passed into adulthood today and by all rights, I was capable of my own decisions now. I felt robbed of everything. I rushed into the room and knelt down beside this man who wasn't my father. We'd sat together against this very wall during a time I didn't understand but when I had first realized my parents didn't love each other like they should have. They had messed up my whole life in their own sick way of chasing happiness and obligations.

"Da," I said. "Daddy, are you okay?" I wanted him to look at me, to see just how far the simple word 'daddy' would run anguish through him.

He reached for my hand, which I drew back before he touched me. "Annae…." He whispered my name as if it were a candle lighting the darkness. He started to rise, but his body had realized he'd become an old man, not an agile youth any longer.

He was the stranger in my house now. Sickening dread twisted in my stomach as an instinctive plan took hold. "Where's your cane, Da. I'll get it then I'll help you up."

He waved his hand, indicating by the door. Mother saw it first and picked it up. I snatched it from her and spun around and raised the cane over my head. My grip tightened on the ferrule. Surprise entered his eyes as he tried to shrink back away from me.

I had enough of strangers in my house. Before I'd been too young, too afraid, to do much about it. But now…

With all the force I could muster, I brought the cane's rounded handle down on his bad leg. He had twisted so it impacted with the side of his knee. At the sound of an explosive pop, I expected a howl of pain. Instead, he only grunted as he made a grab for the cane. I swung it away and around, this time coming down on his back. I attacked, remembering all the moves I'd mimicked after watching him teaching the boys. I bet he'd wished he was still wearing his armor. He moved as though he had it on, as though it were natural for him to let the protective metal take the weapon blow. I struck him again across the front of his chest near his shoulder. I'd been aiming for his face. With each blow, I wished that the cane would break, drive splinters deep under his skin.

"Annae!" Mother screamed as she seized the cane. "He's the one who's taken care of you all your life."

"Taken care of me in a lie." I released the cane. "Who are you really?"

He accepted the cane from my mother and stood up. He didn't put any weight on the leg I'd hit, but rather hopped over to his chair to sit down. A dribble of blood ran from the corner of his mouth and for half a moment I felt guilty about it. He leaned on the table as though it would give him strength.

"Steigan."

The blow felt physical and knocked the wind from my lungs. "As in Saint Steigan? Is this some sort of jest?" I asked.

"Dominari Steigan," he corrected as if the distinction in title made any difference to me.

I ignored his weak protest and continued, "That makes you a liar and a murderer! Who are you that you think you can pretend to be my father, pretend that everything will be all right, pretend that we're a family? Liar!"

He shook his head. He'd been the one who put me on the track to be a Temple historian. Now that I'd had my Independence Blessing, I could begin my final studies to moving into that position. I remembered my lessons on The Breaking and Reunification. Had he been mocking me, knowing that he wasn't only helping me study, but he had actually been responsible for that chapter? For that matter, he'd helped Queen Keteria destroy Lilinar. Not to mention the Cauldron of Life. Would my brother still be alive if Mom had been able to go and drink from the springs at the Cauldron?

"You cannot possibly be him. My mother wouldn't let someone that insane into our house to live with us." Yet even as I said the words, I realized that she had and that her carousing and wild nights had been her way of numbing this knowledge from her mind. All the shameful pieces were coming together.

I found myself backing toward the door.

"Annae, you can't tell anyone," Mom said. "It would be very dangerous if the wrong person found out he was here."

I looked at my mother, wondering when her sanity had fled. In my brief reflection, I realized that all of her actions were crazy. "So you're just going to keep pretending? Keep on protecting him?"

She averted her eyes and it was all the confirmation I need. I'd been let in on the lie my parents held dear, but it would remain intact regardless of my feelings. I ran out of the house then and spent a good portion of the night walking the streets in the moonlight. When I was so tired and about to collapse, I returned home. The lights were out but I heard Dad's – no, Steigan's door click softly closed. He had waited up until he knew I was safely home. Too tired to feel renewed anger, I wondered if he would wake me in the morning for class like he'd done for so long, but the sun was high when I woke.

I packed my things and went to find my mother in the kitchen. She sat at the table, a pot of strickleberry tea in the center and an unused cup on each side of her. She wasn't even dressed yet, but it looked like she'd been up for hours. Had she been waiting?

She motioned for me to sit, even started reaching for one of the cups to fill. Did she really think that we would sit around and make things better over a cup of tea?

I shook my head, gripping onto the handles of my bag tighter. "I'm going to go live at the school, in the dormitories, while I finish my final studies," I said. "I need to understand all this and I can't do it here with you two fighting all the time."

"I can tell him to leave. He raised you until you were of age; his debt to you is paid."

"And what will we do for a living?" I asked. "Until I have income from the Temple, we still need his help. Meanwhile, he can pay for me to stay at the dormitories. If Saint Steigan wants to repent by taking care of us, let him. He was right, Ma. Find happiness where you will and let him wallow in his own self-pity."

She wanted to refute this, but her eyes confirmed the truth of my statement. She gripped the cup before her and looked down into it. When she didn't say anything further, I left the house and didn't look back.

Only after I finished my final studies for the Temple and started my apprenticeship did I realized that I had never seen Steigan come around the school grounds to teach the boys like he once had. I also noticed that he no longer attended Temple services at the castle. As I'd walk down the marble steps toward the sanctuary inside Dubinshire Castle, I'd look over the crowd for a sign of him. In realizing that this was becoming a familiar ritual to me, I began to wonder when my anger had abated.

"Why doesn't he come?" I asked Mom before morning service one day. "I feel I'm keeping him from worshiping the Goddess."

She gave me a weak smile. "The Goddess lives in his heart. He doesn't need this --" She raised her hands to indicate the stone Temple around them. "-- to worship Her. This is all fancy dressings."

"Is that why he could grow a religion, then turn around and destroy it?"

She shook her head. "I don't know if we'll ever have the answer to that." She reached out and tucked a strand of black hair back behind my ear while giving a sad smile. She too had her own questions that would never be fully known. I began to wonder if playing the role of my father had become more than just a way to repent, but a tomb for all the things he'd done wrong.

We spoke no more about him until she came one day to have Sapere Hyrin approve an appellate splitting their marriage. Since everyone thought he was my father, Searn, and they were legally married, documents had to be prepared to separate them. I served as my mother's witness stating that things had not been good between them and that they even slept in different rooms.

The next day she married Nikael.

Two cycles went by. I took an official position as an assistant to the historian who served under Sapere Hyrin's secretary. I'd taken an interest in The Breaking and Reunification and studied that period in-depth, even asking Holy Sapere Kelan to borrow books from the library at New Lilinar for me. When questioned about my fascination, even though twenty cycles had passed since it had happened, I replied with the truth: I'd been born during the turmoil and my father, Searn, had been one of the warriors fighting to save Lilinar. I'd learned my real father had been a nephew to King Cirello and cousin to Queen Keteria, who was said to have fallen in love with Dominus Steigan until he was made a saint by the Temple. That action alone was said to have snapped her mind and allowed the magic to distort her mental stability. As I reviewed my mother's own crazy life, I wondered if every woman involved with Steigan had been driven mad. I discovered that Searn had once had land and a title to his name. The more I learned, the more I wanted to know from the one man who could tell me: Dominari Steigan.

Not everyone was happy about me searching for the facts. Sapere Hyrin tried to warn me off first. "His identity must remain secret," he said, though he wouldn't tell me why it was so important. It just was. But no one could keep me from studying my chosen period. I wanted very badly to travel to New Lilinar to read their version of history because I knew somewhere in it was the truth.

"Study the history of the Temple in your own town," I was told. "Don't raise the demons of the dead."

I smiled and replied, "We must study all history if we are to learn from it. We wouldn't want the same thing happening to our Temple."

"Your questions are stirring old animosities," Holy Sapere Kelan noted later with foreboding.

One day, while taking instruction from Sapere Hyrin and his secretary about work needing to be done, Holy Sapere Kelan burst into the room. "Hyrin, the Holy Sapere of New Lilinar approaches. Lord Freygorio says 'tis time."

Hyrin nodded and turned to me. "Annae, 'tis time you should take to the library."

I felt my stomach tighten. I had only one shot to persuade my superiors that I should be allowed in the diplomatic session and not relegated to the library. "Holy Sapere Tanold is a cousin to me. I realize that there are some things that cannot be said, but I should like to see him. I do not even know what he looks like, this removed family of mine."

Hyrin and Kelan glanced at each other, then Kelan nodded. "Assist me then. We will need an unbiased account of the dealings today," he said.

I could barely keep from jumping up and down. I would now get to see the man who St. Steigan hated almost as badly as the Holy Sapere before Tanold, the Holy Sapere which Steigan had killed.

Lord Freygorio didn't look surprised by my presence as we entered his audience chamber. Maybe he didn't realize my relationship to Holy Sapere Tanold. I took a seat near the window where I'd have adequate light for writing as well as for viewing my cousin without having to squint. A couple of the windows had been opened, allowing for a breeze in the room, and the black and gold curtains rustled enough to sweep back and forth in small circles over the stone tile floor and against the back of my chair. I opened my journal across my lap and took out a quill and inkwell. I had no place to set my ink, so I held it, capped for the moment, in one hand.

My heart beat as each moment pressed on. Freygorio chatted with Kelan, who stood beside his lord's chair. Soon, I heard footsteps outside in the hallway. Then with a click, the old wood door swung open. An impressive line of domini in blue and gold entered the room, followed by saperes in their white robes. Then, surrounded by four additional domini, a man entered. His sunburst collar swayed as he walked and it reflected the light coming in through the windows off the gold trim as if it were sunlight itself. Off his shoulders hung long golden braids which reached almost to the floor. His brown hair was starting to show signs of gray. As the line of domini and saperes split, they formed a protective aisle all the way up to the base of Freygorio's dais. Considering that Freygorio only had two of his own guards in the room, I wondered if he felt any worry.

I uncapped my ink and made a note of this. I realized as I did so, that if Tanold ordered his domini to attack, my notes about Freygorio being outnumbered in the siege had to make it out. The truth had to be made known. I would have to escape no matter the cost.

Tanold made a slight bow. "My good Lord Freygorio, I thank you for granting me an audience. Please accept this as a token of my appreciation."

Tanold glanced toward a short, round sapere who I now noticed carried a box with him. The sapere shuffled forward and started to extend the box toward Freygorio.

Freygorio shook his head. "Keep your false text. We have no need for those lies here in Dubinshire."

"Olierex," Tanold said softly and the sapere stepped back into line. "So 'tis true then: the Lord of Dubinshire still has his future-sight."

"Or I am just aware of what kind of treachery you would try to sneak into my kingdom."

I gasped even as I wrote the words as fast as I could. I chanced a glance up to see my cousin's reaction, if this would cause the attack I was so sure was coming. As for future-sight, I wasn't quite sure of the meaning behind the words, only that there was some history between the two men which hadn't been recorded in any documentation I knew.

"I need no tokens in exchange for this audience," Freygorio continued. "Some rulers understand they must be accessible for the needs of their people."

Now I really couldn't help looking up at this intentional slam. I needed to know how Tanold would react.

But Tanold barely let his eyes narrow, keeping a perfect façade of peace on his face. "As you wish. I will make my request and be on my way. I seek to know the whereabouts of my cousin, Searn Bytherhourn."

"You think I would know where he is."

"I think a man such has yourself who is accessible for the needs of his people would be familiar with his citizens as well."

Freygorio smiled at this barbed remark. "Your cousin is a broken, crippled man. I doubt you would find any resemblance to the person you use to know."

"I should like to be the judge of that," Tanold said. "I have important news to relate to him."

"I cannot allow it. He has come here for sanctuary, to live out his days in peace, and I have given it."

"I have seen the ghost of Saint Steigan walking around

the castle ruins," Tanold yelled. "I have sent domini inside the walls of the abandoned city, only to have them return witless. I must know that he has no part in this."

"I assure you: Searn cannot travel such a distance any more, nor would he able to outrun your domini let alone frighten them to insanity."

"I must see for myself." Tanold's voice was steady now. I could tell he was not going to let up until permission was granted and if it weren't given, he would take to the streets going from house to house.

"What would you do if you came across Saint Steigan?" I asked, the words out of my mouth before I'd had a chance to contemplate them.

The line of domini and saperes parted as Tanold turned to me. "Is this for the record, Historian?"

"Yes," I gasped.

His eyes were so bitterly dark and time hardened. "Were I to find him and he were not dead already, I would sever his hands from his arms with his own sword so he could no longer raise it against anyone, then cauterize the wounds so he would not bleed out. That would be far too fast of a death for him. I would drive skews through his muscles so he would know what my heart has felt for twenty cycles. I would smash the bones in both his legs so he could never stand against anyone ever again. I would remove half of his tongue right down the center so he would know what it feels like to have words unsaid. Is this sickening you?"

I realized I'd dropped my gaze, unable to look any longer at this man who didn't know he was talking to family. "No," I said, looking back at him, "I understand how you feel." Steigan had taken Tanold's sister, Queen Keteria, from him much in the same way that he'd taken my parents from me. I stood up as I realized that my mother's feelings were not the same as they would have been if my true father had lived and been part of our family. I had a chance to avenge my father, right here, right now, with my distant cousin as a spearhead. "What other torture would you have?"

"I would heat the metal armor he loves so dearly and bond it to his skin so he would never be able to shed himself of the past and the scars he put on so many."

Freygorio shifted in his chair, crossing one leg over the other. "I cannot help noticing that you have taken up his blue and gold armor across the ranks of your guards. One would almost think this is a veneration of your hateful obsession, to make all those protecting you look just like him. Do you worry you will forget his face?"

Tanold turned so fast his robes swished. He walked along the aisle of domini, pointed at them as he went. "I did this so we would never forget the traitor in our midst. The domini of New Lilinar are naught but lowly guards now. They are not nobility. They are not meant to be rulers. Only the Holy Sapere and his divine connection with the Goddess should ever lead the people."

"Is that what Rivic wanted? Or is that just another lie you tell your people so they will worship at your feet?"

"You are blind, sitting here at the very site of original destruction. Cling to your superstition." Tanold turned back to me. "Historian, mark this down that I have heard from the Goddess Herself that Dubinshire shall fall because of their ruler's inability to disavow magic and assure that 'tis never restored."

Freygorio turned on his throne so that he could lean back a little more. He crossed his arms over his chest. "Historian, mark it down as he says."

Tanold looked shocked that Lord Freygorio would back the command. I grabbed my book and inkwell, scribbling quickly what I had just heard.

When I had finished, Freygorio said, "I do believe that

you were telling her about what you would do with Saint Steigan if you found him alive. Continue."

A wary look passed between Tanold and Freygorio, but the Lord of Dubinshire just waved his hand. Tanold's cold, dark eyes came back to me. "Did you know he had the ability to call a unicorn? I would have him summon his beast from the forest and use my domini to catch it and slay the unicorn before him. Then I would take the horn from it and sew it to his forehead so he would forever know that what he holds dear is gone. Each night I would chain him to hang from the walls in the room where my sister sleeps in her eternal spell."

It all seemed like a fair and just punishment to me. The sudden anger rising within me at that thought brought shameful tears to my eyes. "I will take you to him," I said.

"Annae," Kelan protested.

Tanold gasped and his mouth gaped as he looked from Kelan and back to me. "Annae." He whispered my name, like evil curling temptingly around a wavering man's heart. The sound from his lips held no love like it had when Steigan had uttered it. "Annae Bytherhourn?"

"I am the daughter of Searn Bytherhourn."

At that moment, I saw the darkness within Tanold, the serpent lying so deeply, coiled, waiting. This man standing before me, holding up false words as the Goddess' truth, delighted in the demise of magic. He would forbid it from ever returning to the world. My father had stood beside Dominari Steigan to prevent this disaster. Had my father still been alive and Tanold had come to see him, it would not end well for Searn. If Tanold realized the current deception, it would be even worse.

I felt myself shaking with fear as I stepped toward Tanold. "I will take you to visit Searn when you have cleansed your soul of anything the Goddess would damn you for. Restore Lilinar. Restore our great family. Restore our beliefs. Until then, I will not lead you to the man who raised me so that you can betray him. Nothing good is in your heart."

I walked down the aisle created from Tanold's men, fully expecting him to give the order to kill me. The nasty, little, round sapere stuck out his foot as I passed as if to trip me. I stepped over his leg and kept walking. My trembling fingers could barely work the latch on the door to open it. It released, I went through to safety, and as soon as it closed behind me, I ran.

I didn't realize where I was going until I neared the house where I'd grown up. There was a royal coach outside. I was still down the street when I saw Hyrin come out, followed closely behind by Steigan. Had Hyrin come to warn Steigan or betray him?

"Da," I called out. I waved my arms as I shouted.

Steigan climbed into the carriage behind Hyrin.

"Da!" I yelled again.

The coach rolled forward and headed down the street. Sapere Hyrin had come to Dubinshire with Steigan and now they were leaving. They didn't seem to be turning back toward the castle, but rather heading away. Was this how it ended? Would I ever see him again?

Having felt Holy Sapere Tanold's anger and knowing how many people hated St. Steigan for destroying the Cauldron of Life, as well as blaming him for there being no magic left in the world, I grew more curious about why those who were loyal to Dominari Steigan remained so. What was it about him? Why had my own emotions betrayed me? Why had Kelan worried when I said I would take Tanold to Steigan while Freygorio had only smiled? My account of the meeting surmised at some of these things, but they were only my best guess. I kept my eyes cast downward as I slid my reporting across the desk to Kelan and he read it.

"I hope you see now," Kelan said, "why 'tis important for

Dubinshire to break from New Lilinar and why you must focus your attentions on Dubinshire rather than the devastation of Lilinar."

"I am sorry, Holy Sapere," I said barely glancing up for a brief exchange of looks between us. "The Goddess placed me in the Temple at Lilinar and chose to help me and my mother escape. 'Tis part of my personal history. I survived The Breaking. Not everyone was so lucky." I felt myself getting braver now. "My research and writings are a memorial to them. I shall not stop."

I clung not only to history, but to the faith that came with it. A few months into the new cycle after I'd started as assistant historian, I became a priestess. I remember dancing and twirling, spinning around the main hall of Dubinshire Castle, enjoying the sensation of the new, golden priestess belt jangling around my hips, until I was so dizzy I thought I might fall. I came to a sudden stop in someone's arms. Where a moment ago my head had been abuzz with celebration, being caught by this man snapped me back to my senses. I first noticed his domini armor, then I looked up into beautiful jade colored eyes set into his perfect face framed by light brown hair, and my wits only lasted a moment before he sent my world whirling again.

"Milady," he said as he interlaced one hand with mine while his other came to my hip. He twirled around, dancing through the room with me. It felt like just the two of us spinning and spinning as the bards played. His strength, his boldness, the gentle look in his eyes... I loved everything about him from that moment.

"I am Ral Chitanik," he said.

"A pleasure to meet you, Dominus," I returned. "I am –"

"I know who you are, Annae Bytherhourn." He smiled as he swept me around the floor and I felt as if I were floating. "I hope you forgive me for my interruption, but watching you celebrate and dance finally gave me courage enough to introduce myself."

I hoped he couldn't feel the tingles running over my skin. "Since you disrupted this dance, I may expect another, one where you ask me properly beforehand."

"You would require me to work up my courage twice, especially after all the fears running through my head of missing you to begin with?"

"You mean a dominus like yourself didn't fully anticipate making that suave catch?"

Goddess, how his smile just made me melt!

"Quite the contrary."

"Then maybe you shouldn't let me go."

He wanted to say something, but he held back the words. I tried to think of something to break the silence between us. I only found the most obvious of questions which I didn't want to ask but did as the quiet between us lengthened. "I haven't seen you around and I thought I knew most of the domini."

"I just became one. Inducted two nights ago."

"So you trained here in Dubinshire too?"

"I did. Your father was one of my first trainers. He's a brilliant teacher."

I found myself looking around the hall for Steigan's face as Ral took me for another circle around the room. It felt so vacant, this mass of people all here to celebrate the induction of the new priestess and celebration of new rankings, yet to not have my father here. Especially with Ral making me recall all the nights we spent together studying.

"You know," he said, "I use to watch him bringing you to your classes. You'd kiss his cheek then laugh as you ran off for your lessons. He'd stay behind and watch until you were no longer in sight. I knew what a strong and kind man your father was, but to watch how he adored you showed a whole other side to him. I knew the two of you shared a special bond."

I felt the tiles beneath my feet. I'd come back down to earth. I wanted to tell Ral that Steigan wasn't my father and what he was really like, but I couldn't rebuke Ral's words. What would he think if he knew Steigan was a coward and had run away to hide in Montikovert until Tanold quit his search for Searn Bytherhourn and returned to New Lilinar?

Ral continued, "There was a Springsday Festival where you were standing at the fence cheering for your father to win."

"I always did that."

"But I didn't always know that. I pretended that you were cheering for me instead. I came close to winning that year."

"Close?"

"Most everyone had been tagged out by your father three times. I hadn't been tagged yet. I knew I just needed to wait. As the field cleared and your father and I circled each other, I realized that you were cheering for your dad who was leaning far too much on his cane. How could I defeat one of the proudest men I knew, one of my very own teachers, and let him falter in the eyes of his daughter?"

"I remember that. You tripped."

"I pretended to trip. After he tagged me, I went to gather my first ribbon from Leloran and told her that I conceded the fight. I walked off the field as another wave of boys rushed out."

"My father thought you had twisted your ankle."

"'Tis what I told Leloran."

"But you did it for me?"

I received a smile as my answer. His green eyes sparkled. On the outside, he looked nothing like Steigan, but the emotions on his face were so similar.

Our song ended and Ral released me. He bowed. "'Tis been a pleasure, milady."

My heart thundered more than it had when he first snatched me mid-spin. I had told him to never let me go and now he was about to walk away. If he did, it would cripple my heart. I felt tears enter my eyes. "I miss him." Don't make me miss you too, I wanted to add.

The bards started playing the next song, a slow beat full of emotional longing. My nose prickled as the tears started to flow.

Ral's brilliant smile fell away to concern. "May I have this dance?" he asked.

I practically fell against him as his arms encircled me once more. His armor felt cool on my cheek.

"What happened between the two of you?" Ral asked.

"I grew up."

"You never cried over losing him, did you?"

I only shook my head.

Throughout the evening and over the next few days, Ral continued telling stories of adventure, of dreams, and of the sword challenges at the Springsday Festivals. Within every memory Ral evoked for me, I found a man who had always wanted the best for me and for my mother.

It didn't take long for rumors to spread through the Temple that Ral and I were a couple. Even shorter was the time it took for him to propose, me to accept, and us to be handbound in marriage.

Ral and I stood before Holy Sapere Kelan, our hands tied together with a soft gold cord. Sapere Hyrin would've been happy to do this for us, but I had wanted the Holy Sapere himself to officiate. Holy Sapere Kelan didn't often perform marriage ceremonies and convincing him to do this was a rare honor. Accomplishing this difficult task myself made me appreciate all Steigan had done for me in the past. He barely ever had to say, "Please," to get what he needed.

At the ceremony, my mother and Nikeal sat nearby with Ral's parents and friends, and I realized with sadness that Steigan wasn't here to celebrate with us. It felt wrong. At the moment in my life when I should have felt happiest, I was overcome with regret. Did he hate me for striking him with the cane? How could I even begin to apologize? I should have gone to see him when I realized he was back in Dubinshire.

Ral leaned in to kiss me and I saw something flutter passed my cheek. A second later, a light weight landed in my hair. Then another. Ral and I both looked up into a shower of strickleberry petals. Above, on the walk around the Temple, was Steigan leaning over sprinkling the petals on us. "May the Goddess bless you both, always," he said. Then he blew a kiss to us and disappeared from sight.

"He'll never forgive me," I told Ral later that night when I admitted everything to him, including my father's true identity. "I was beyond cruel."

Ral smiled, that pleasing smile that melted my heart like only he could do. "I think he already has. Besides, I use to beat him with a stick too, remember? He's probably use to it."

I wanted to laugh, but ended up crying. Ral held me until I fell asleep.

I left early the next morning before my obligations at the Temple called me to duty. Holding my skirt up slightly, I ran down the street and hoped that Steigan still followed the same route he'd done for so many cycles. I saw him in the baker's shop and smiled. The Goddess was on my side today and this was the right thing to do. I pushed open the door and overhead their conversation.

"Aye, I can take the increase to four coins in each loaf, but if you increase it to five, I'll be spillin' dough out o'the pan."

"Thank you. I know you're trying your best. What about Mykgreg? Do you think he'd wrap a coin with the fruit?

"Mykgreg's an honest man, even if stogie about his fruit. I'll take the extra and get him to wrap it. The fewer who know, the -- "

The baker had noticed me walk in on them and it was only as his gaze glanced between the two of us that Steigan turned.

"Very good," Steigan recovered. "Do that and have it sent. And my usual for next week, can you deliver it to the house? Don't get around like I use to."

I realized then that the cane was gone, but around his leg was a metal contraption that moved with him as he walked. The brace looked uncomfortable, but a brilliant piece of his craftsmanship.

"Be glad to, Searn," the baker replied.

Steigan walked toward me, the metal clicking as he moved, but he didn't look directly at me.

"Da?" The word cracked from my throat.

Steigan paused, a small hiccup in his step that he had to regain due to the stiffness of the brace, but he kept going. I turned and followed him out the door.

"Da, wait..."

He stopped, his head tipping back slightly. When had his hair turned so gray? "I'm sorry," he said though he didn't turn to face me. "I had no right to be at your ceremony the other day."

I bypassed his apology. "You're the one who's been sending coins to Mom. You know, she almost broke her tooth on the first one."

His chest shook, a single laugh or possibly a choke. "Her sailor has not left port in some time. Taken to gambling and drinking, I've heard."

"So what business is that of yours?"

He turned quickly, a movement belittling the fact he was getting older. "I made a promise to your dad. A promise to take care of you and Centhya. I may be a murderer and a liar in your book, but don't make me an oathbreaker too."

"No, you wouldn't break your word, would you?"

His eyes looked tired. "You'll have to be your own judge of that. Only you can tell me how good my word is." He raised his leg as if it took heaving it first to get him to start walking. "I am glad that you and your mother have gotten onto better terms now."

I rushed around him and threw my arms around him to give him a hug. I wanted to take away all the anguish I'd caused him, but he already held so much tragedy that I wasn't sure where my sorrow ended and his pain began. "I'm sorry, Da. I've been foolish. Can you forgive me?"

"There's nothing for me to forgive. You're the one that was wronged, not me."

"Come to dinner tonight, Da. Ral would love to visit with you and you look like you need a good home cooked meal or fifty. Please?"

Steigan showed up that evening carrying a strickleberry pie.

Steigan and Ral chatted like warrior comrades. Finally, Ral excused himself for a moment and I asked Steigan if he wanted to step out into the gardens.

We walked out to the stone wall which surrounded the garden and Steigan watched several children playing out on the cobblestone street beyond the outer edge of my garden. One boy was getting blindfolded and spun around by two other boys while three others waited. "Cannot run, cannot hide, he's at your back and not on your side." They released the blindfolded boy. "Bloody saint!" they all screamed before scattering.

Steigan gave a muffled chuckle as the blindfolded boy

crouched, tightened his hold on his wooden sword, and started listening for the children around him.

"How do you feel about that?" I asked, knowing the game the boys were playing had been created because of St. Steigan. The butterflies hitting my stomach told me that maybe I should have waited a bit before approaching such a potentially delicate situation.

He surprised me with a smile. "Had I known at the time what I know now, I would've framed the game a little differently and I wouldn't have let Lord Ithanes goad me. But I think it's a game the kids will still be playing a thousand years from now. It'll deepen the legend. So it's good. I hope one day your children play the Bloody Saint game."

I knew so much about what history had recorded about the life of St. Steigan, but so little of the emotions behind the events. If I wanted all the facts, I'd have to start by mending what had happened between us. "I'm sorry if I injured you further," I said, indicating his leg wrapped in the iron brace.

"In truth, you did me a service that day."

I turned to him, feeling the shocked look on my face, but he rested his hands against the stone wall and leaned into it looking out over the gardens. "I'd come to rely on the cane far too much. My muscles were weakening. This brace has forced me to rethink my healing and has strengthened all my muscles again." He glanced at me now. "I only wear the brace when I go out now to keep me steady."

"So at home you're walking all day without it and without a cane?"

He nodded. "I wouldn't have gotten this far without you."

Goddess! His words were so carefully chosen. They left me unable to respond, discarded me to sink even deeper into the quicksand of my guilt.

"I chose Ral because he reminded me so much of you," I

said, wondering if I could bluster the conversation any further.

Steigan smiled, a small chuckle under his breath, and nodded his head. "He's a good choice. An honorable man."

"I wanted to let you know that." I rested my hand on his. "I appreciate how you've always taken care of me and my mother, and I'm sorry with how things ended. You went beyond anything you needed to do."

"I made a promise."

"I know and I release you from your vow. Mom and I are both taken care of now. 'Tis time we released you from your obligation so that you can live your life."

His eyes closed and opened slowly, but not a flicker of emotion crossed his face. "I won't be around forever. Let me help you while I can. Besides," he said reaching to his belt, "if I can't give this to you, then who will I give it to."

He pulled out a pouch of money and held it out toward me.

"I can't."

Gently, Steigan took my hand and put the leather pouch in my hand. "Take it. You and Ral can buy something exciting with it. Or save it until you have children, and when you spend it on them, tell them it's from their doting grandfather."

I couldn't help my smile. "Doting, huh?" But my heart felt the daggers of his warning about not being around forever. His leg might be healing, but did he know the rest of him was failing? Was he trying to tell me he felt death's shadow over him?

He looked back at the gardens and was silent.

I leaned against the wall so I could look at him. "Were you friends with my father?"

"We were more than that." His eyes grew sad. "Searn

helped me when no one else would have. I owe him my life in more ways than one. He was my family."

"Will you tell me about him? I know about The Breaking and Reunification, but I don't know how he played his part in it. What were you really trying to do? What did he believe in so much that he died for it?"

"Why don't I start out telling you about who he was before we get into the intricacies of history?" He put his arm around my shoulders and started guiding me back to the house. "History is colored by the victors."

"And its truth comes from the lives of the common man. Dominari Steigan wasn't common, which is why you chose to hide under my father's name."

"I chose to celebrate your father with life. He deserves for his stories to finally be told. Come on, let's go inside."

That night, he enthralled Ral with tales of heroic deeds and I scribbled notes furiously, hoping to capture a trace of my father and the man who had pretended to be my father.

He said that my father found him along the roadside while returning to Lilinar from a hunting trip with his uncle, Merkor, and his cousin, Prince Tanold. Steigan had been found dressed in domini armor, which they first thought had been stolen. When no dominus stepped forward to claim the armor, the mystery deepened. It was as though Steigan had just appeared there.

Searn took Steigan in and gave him a home, believing that they were cousins too. They had similar looks between them, but Searn's shorter hair distinguished him from Steigan.

In trying to regain his memory, Steigan had worked with Princess Keteria, temporary High Maege for the Temple while the official High Maege, my mother, had been pregnant with me. King Cirello, father of Keteria and Tanold, had died in accident at the Temple. It was said magic had addled his mind and caused his insanity. Following the King's death, Keteria took over as Queen of Lilinar.

"But how did Searn die?" I insisted finally.

Steigan got up and started heading for the door. "The hour grows late and that's another tale." He paused with his hand on the latch and I saw him give me a half smile. "How does history say he died?"

I wanted to stamp my foot. I felt like a little girl again, answering questions for him when we studied my lessons and he wanted me to riddle my own way out. "History doesn't say he died."

"Exactly." He pulled the door closed behind him.

I stared at the closed door for a moment, then it hit me. I ran for the door and threw it open. "History says Saint Steigan died."

Steigan waved back at me and kept walking down the road.

The next day, Lord Freygorio came to visit me in the library at Dubinshire Castle. "I have a special request for you," he said.

I knew one did not easily turn away the Lord of Dubinshire. "Milord?"

"I hear that you and your father have had a reconciliation."

"We have, Milord."

He nodded slowly, thoughtfully. "I should like to see you become a historian for the Onim."

"The Onim?"

His eyes widened for but a moment in surprise. Then he smiled. "Then I set you to your first task. Discover the Onim. Then, when you understand you mission, send a letter to the Council of Lords to request funds. It will be a delicate matter, so take heed to make sure you understand the full situation before making your request."

That was how I first heard of the Onim.

At home, I asked Ral if he knew about the Onim. A scowl darkened his face, then he admitted, "I know your father has been tracking the lineage of several families. I remember him coming into my house when I was a young boy and meeting with my parents. My mother lined out our family tree in a book he had brought with him."

"That doesn't sound like much of a secret group. Why wouldn't he just get the records from the Temple historians?"

"Because if he accessed the birth registers at the Temple, there would be note of him accessing the archives," Ral answered. "Maybe he's keeping track of something specific."

"That's not enough information."

"I know my father meets with Steigan and several other domini families several times each cycle. He's been doing this for a long time. It could have something to do with the Onim." Ral thought for a moment, then added, "I also remember Dad coming home from one of these meetings with a book. He wrapped it in several layers of oil cloth and leather and buried it deep beneath the garden gate that very night. When I asked him about it, he said he would explain it to me when I got older."

"But neither he nor Steigan has said anything to you about this Onim?" I asked.

"No, but I will ask my dad. Lord Freygorio would not have come to you with this task if it weren't important."

During the next cycle, Steigan and I grew closer, like an actual father and daughter, much like it had been when I was younger. I never asked him about the Onim though. Our relationship needed the time to heal, not to be injured by me confronting him about another of his secrets. When I became pregnant, Ral was beside himself with excited stress and Steigan stepped quickly into being the doting grandfather.

"I want to name him Steigan," I told him one day when he escorted me on my morning walk through the gardens. I rubbed my palm over my round belly, feeling a little kick beneath my palm.

"Better come up with some girl names instead."

"A girl?" I took his hand and placed it where I had just felt the kick. "No, 'tis going to be a boy."

"I wouldn't be so certain. Besides, Steigan's probably cursed. No one bearing that name will ever fair well, I'm afraid. Best to let it fade into obscurity."

"Oh, come on. There's more to a person than their name. You of all people should know that."

He shrugged. "Doesn't matter. Steigana isn't very charming, so you'll just have to find another."

My mother barely knew I was pregnant. The fine clothes she once wore were turning to rags and her graying hair rarely seemed combed. Worse, it seemed like she often had a new bruise or two. I wasn't the naive girl I'd once been. I knew what was happening. I begged Mom to get an appellate to break the handbond between her and Nikael, but she said that it'd never be granted. She claimed that she'd angered the wrong people in the Temple when she'd broken off from their beloved St. Steigan. Truly, he was always among friends when he was with loyal believers of the Temple, but I knew she was more afraid of Nikael. I told her that Ral and I would take her in, but she refused.

After not hearing from her for nearly a fortnight, I went to her house late one afternoon when I knew Nikael would've left for the tavern already. She opened the door, then tried to close it in my face. I stuck my foot in the door to keep it ajar. I pushed harder until she backed off a little and she looked out the gap at me again. Her face was swollen, her lower lip still bloody. One eye had an old yellowing bruise and the other had a fresh mark.

"Mother, come with me now."

"Go away, Annae. He mustn't find you here. It would be bad." Her voice was a bare raspy whisper.

I knew she was insinuating that Nikael would hurt me and harm the baby. "I'll get Ral, then. We'll come back for you."

"No. Please, just go. Leave me alone."

"Are you just going to let him beat you until you're dead?"

"If I go with you, he'll come looking for me and no one I'm with will be safe."

"That's such a lie. You think the drunken sod can take on Ral?"

"He's got friends."

I knew what she meant: burly sailing buddies who were also out of work and probably just as drunk and surly as Nikael. Ral was a good guy, a kind heart, but he hadn't been battle tested. I knew this and so did Mom. He also didn't have a whole lot of friends, not like Nikael did. But I couldn't just leave my mother to his fists either.

"I'll think of something." I pulled my foot from the door and started down the walkway. I cried angry tears before I'd even reached the road. I needed someone who could take on Nikael without fear, someone who could hold his own against one or many without a flicker of emotion, someone who would care about my mother enough to come to her rescue. I knew the answer, but I didn't know how to ask for the favor.

I found myself on Steigan's doorstep without ever actually formulating a plan about what I was going to say. He opened the door, saw my tears, and instantly his whole body braced for whatever was coming. He put his hands on my shoulders and pulled me close. "What is it, Annae? What's wrong? Is the baby okay?"

"Daddy," I sobbed against him. "Daddy, you've got to stop him."

"Who?"

"Nikael. He's beating Mom."

Steigan ushered me into his house and had me sit down before he grabbed his sword belt from the back of a chair and strapped it around his waist. "You wait here. Is he at your mother's house now?"

"No, he was at the tavern a few minutes ago."

"Stay here." The door slammed shut behind him. Chills took me. I finally had to go stand in front of the kitchen fire and rub my arms to try to warm myself. It didn't help. Nor did the baby kicking me, jabbing its little foot up into my ribcage.

"You want out to take him on too, don't you?" I said, rubbing my belly.

The door opened awhile later and Steigan came in with Mother, dragging her along by the arm. He practically tossed her into the chair where I'd been sitting. "Get some rags," he said, already moving to put a pot of water on over the fire. "She's got some broken ribs and probably a fracture in her arm too, not to mention infection setting into several open wounds."

"Oh, by the Goddess, Mother!" I hadn't seen the worst of it when she'd looked out the door at me and I barely recognized her now.

"Look, she's numb, she's not feeling any of this anymore," he shouted at me to break me out of my stupor. Of all the times mother had screamed at him, he'd never raised his voice. He'd never given more than a whimper when I wanted to see his rage. But now, he was angrier than I'd ever seen. "Bleeding saints! I'm going to kill him." Like a charging bull, he started for the door.

"Da, I can't take care of her alone. You've got to help me."

His gaze flickered to the door and for a moment he swayed on his feet as if deciding what to do. Looking at my protruding belly seemed to firm his resolve on what needed done. He removed his sword belt and headed toward his room. "I'd better put this out of my sight or I might just decide to use it."

For the rest of the evening, Steigan cleaned her wounds and bandaged her up. He knelt down beside her and for the first time I realized that he was without his brace. He brushed tendrils of hair back from her face. It still looked battered, but at least it was no longer bloody. "There's my beautiful girl," he told her with a smile.

She looked like she wanted to cry but was completely unable to. "I can only imagine what I look like," she said half turning away from him. "Time is a great equalizer, isn't it?"

"Sooner or later, we all get humbled." He leaned close and put his forehead gently against hers. "But we couldn't have happy celebrations if we didn't have times of sorrow as well."

"Have you ever been happy here?" Her words were so soft I wasn't even sure I heard them correctly.

He held her face in his hands, their heads together, for a couple seconds longer before breaking away. "You need a blanket." He started to get up, but I told him I'd get one. I wanted to hear his answer to mother's question as much as she did. Instead, he took Mom's hand and kissed her fingers.

"I make bad choices, don't I, Steigan?" she said. I realized it was the first time I'd ever heard her call him by his real name.

"Sleep now."

I covered her up with the blanket and carefully tucked the edges in around her. "I should get back to Ral. He'll be wondering where I went."

A sudden heavy knock at the door made me jump.

Steigan was on his feet, his arm reaching across him for his sword which was no longer at his side.

"It's against the wall in the library," he told me quickly.

"Searn!" A familiar voice came. "Is Annae with you?"

"Ral." I picked up my skirts and hurried for the door as fast as a pregnant woman could.

He was in my arms the second the door opened. After a hug, he set me to his side and rushed over for Steigan. He saw Mom lying on the couch and did a double take. "Goddess! Is that your mother?"

"Annae and I have been taking care of her since early this afternoon."

His eyes widened. "Then you don't know."

"Know what?" I asked, stepping forward.

"Nikael is dead. Someone caught him cheating and stabbed him with his own knife."

Fate or karma, I didn't know, but I was glad that Steigan didn't have to go after him. There's no doubt in my mind that Steigan would've put Nikael to a cruel death, branding truth to the rumors of Steigan being a wrathful murderer. Until that moment, I hadn't been certain if he was a killer, but I now knew that if his loved ones were threatened, he'd rise to the occasion. Comparing him to Ral, I now understood the difference between dominus and Dominari.

My mother never had to worry about Nikael again. His debts were another thing. It seemed he'd left accounts all over Dubinshire and Montikovert, not to mention the gambling debts from both towns which the thugs tried to collect. Mom sold the house to take care of the honest debts and moved back in with Steigan to take care of the rest.

I gave birth to a girl, just as Steigan had predicted. We called her Searnette, Sea for short. Steigan didn't say anything, but he approved. Tears gathered in his eyes and he leaned over to hug me and the baby. "Searn would be honored."

I grabbed onto his upper arm, giving it a squeeze. He looked at me and in the unspoken words that passed between us, I knew we were both glad that the truth was exposed.

Over the next cycle, I saw my parents in public more and more. Steigan almost always wore his armor and sword. He committed more time to the Temple acting as a dominus. Of course, with so many people in Dubinshire believing he was Searn, he couldn't use his true title of Dominari, but it didn't seem to bother him any.

Still, they received strange looks, and I suspect that did irritate Steigan. My mother's wild nights in the tavern had recklessly destroyed her image and even though she'd never been with another man other than my true father and Nikael, publicly she was seen as a soiled woman. She followed behind Steigan, always a couple steps back as though she herself felt like she didn't deserve to be equal with him anymore. The resetting of her bones had straightened out her limbs, but her self-esteem and dignity was shattered. I mentioned it to Steigan one night when they'd come for dinner and we took our customary walk in the garden afterward.

"I wonder if an abused woman ever quits looking like a rag doll."

He looked up at the two moons, each nearly full. "Sometimes imagined wounds hurt us more than the true physical ones."

Imagined wounds? But before I had a chance to ask him what he meant by that, he went back into the house.

"My leg is bothering me and 'tis late," he told my mom. "We should head home."

With a nod, she handed Sea back to me and followed Steigan out the door.

Two days later at morning service, Steigan walked in arm-in-arm with a woman I didn't recognize at first. Mom's hair had been cut shorter to her shoulders and she wore a dress of white that seemed to float around her. Mom smiled and laughed as she circulated the room both before and after service. It was like stepping back ten cycles. When I asked her about it, she took my hand and pulled me aside like we were best friends instead of mother and daughter.

"Yesterday after morning service, Steigan took me around the town, treating me like a queen. I swear, he bought me a whole new wardrobe. Most of it won't be finished for a month," she whispered in our huddle.

I feared the cycle was starting anew and I didn't want to see either one of them get hurt again. "Mom..."

"We're getting handbound next week."

"What?" My one word came out slower than her whole sentence. I looked up, searching around the room for where Steigan was. I had too many questions, but not to ask my mother. "Congratulations. I want to go talk to Dad now," I said, trying not to sound too flat or too quick. I broke away from her and headed over to where Steigan was standing by Ral. Steigan made popping sounds with his mouth which had Sea giggling hysterically and kicking her legs.

"Da," I said, grabbing his arm. "You're going to get handbound with Mom again."

Steigan smiled and looked over to where Mom was chatting lively with several women. He leaned close. "First time, actually."

I felt my forehead wrinkle and relax several times as I tried to figure this out. "But why? After all this time..." Where was I going with this sentence?

He took my arm and led me aside from the crowd. "That night after supper at your house, Cen and I went home and we talked late into the night. Way later than old folks like us should be awake. But it cleared the air between us."

I squeezed my fingers into my palms, wishing I could understand. "But why now?"

"I realized that your mother wasn't handbound to me, she was handbound to Searn and I was merely filling a spot. She didn't want a spot filled. She wanted a husband who cherished her."

His incredulous words angered me now. "Gee, really? I wouldn't have figured a woman would want that!"

"Annae, I was in love with a Queen, a woman so far above my station that I never felt like I could be near her let alone touch her. I wanted a wife, I've always wanted a wife and family. Losing Keteria..." He took a deep breath. "Cen filled in the same way I took Searn's place. Neither one of us was bound to be happy under those circumstances."

"So you're marrying her as you?" While his words comforted me, he was leaving something out. He wasn't telling the whole story. I didn't have the right questions to ask, not presently.

His eyes grew serious. "I can't take my real name back. I will marry her under Searn's name, be a devoted husband, and cherish her every day I am able."

"But what about your mission? I once heard you tell Ma that you had a duty to the Goddess that only you could fulfill. What happened to that?"

"That hasn't changed, nor has my love for Queen Keteria."

"I don't understand how those things equal."

"You will. You need to. But not yet. Is it okay, for once, for me to not be ready?" He looked close to tears. "I'm not ready for you to know how deeply I've manipulated your life and think me a monster for it again. I want something good to come of this."

"Da?"

"Your mother has had a rough life and lost so much: magic, Searn, a baby, herself. She needs to be made whole, to find strength in her happiness. I need to know you both can carry on without me when my mission is done here. So I will love her like a queen with my remaining days." He grabbed my hands and held them against his chest. "This is my gift to you. I restore your mother to the person she was, to who she should have been while you were growing up."

"What are you not telling me? You would make a solemn handbonding part of your mission too, as another way to repent?" I almost felt sick at the thought. "I think you seek to break us all, not make us better for it."

"Please, Annae, give me your blessing and your patience. It will all make sense in time."

I stretched up and kissed his cheek. "Then I give you my blessing."

"Thank you." He stepped around me and went over to Mom, putting his arm around her.

Sapere Hyrin performed the handbinding the next day with only me, Ral, and Sea present. Afterwards, there was no big reception, just a quiet supper with a few saperes and domini at the Temple, though Lord Freygorio stopped by for a moment. Afterwards, Steigan stepped outside and whistled. A short time later, a unicorn walked from the woods. Steigan helped Mom onto the unicorn and walked beside her toward their home. I felt like I'd been exposed to a touch of the magic that had once been in the world.

"He's going to give himself away," I whispered to Ral as I listened to the fading hoof beats on the cobblestone road. "Only a Dominari can call a unicorn. If someone sees them, they'll know he's Saint Steigan. What is he thinking?"

Ral tucked me against him with his arm around my shoulders. "'Tis late. No one's going to see. Besides, I don't think he cares about anyone but your mother. He did it for her."

I looked up at him, trying to puzzle out what he was thinking. As Ral watched them go down the road, he added, "He's setting a firm distinction between himself and Searn."

I thought on that for the remainder of the night and discovered the truth within. Steigan had been trying so hard to be Searn so that no one aside from the small circle of people who knew him would find out about him, including me as a child. Now, after all these cycles, he finally found it safer to be himself.

They had a marriage over the next few cycles that remain unmatched by any I've ever seen.

Ral and I gave them two more grandchildren, Vinson and Fawla.

It was after the birth of my son, Vinson, that I learned about the Onim. Ma was holding Vinson when Steigan took his little hand and uncurled the tiny fingers to look at the baby's palm.

"There is no mark," he said to Centhya. She nodded solemnly as if understanding something he had left unspoken.

He turned to me, still taken to bed after the long delivery. "I was afraid of this. With magic gone from the world, Rivic's enchantment isn't surfacing."

"Rivic's enchantment?" I asked.

"The birthmark I bear on my palm." He sat down on the edge of the bed on the other side from where Ral sat. "Your son should have the birthmark. He is a direct descendant of Rivic. Any boys that Searnette bears will not have it. You will need to keep track of your children and their families for as long as you are able, then pass that task on to them and their children. The lineage must be recorded."

I knew that was important and about the prophecy of

Lady Alityka being reborn when the golden birthmark appeared.

"It was hard to be sure if the birthmark was still appearing," Dad continued, "since most of Rivic's line resides now in New Lilinar. Vinson is the first boy born who I know for certain should have the torch."

He held his arms out and Mom got up and carried Vinson to his grandfather. She lay Vinson into Steigan's cradling hold, then put her hand on his shoulder. Steigan looked down at the baby and rubbed his big hand over the short tufts of Vinson's black hair. "I wanted you to be a historian, Annae, because I knew there was a burdensome task I would need someone to carry on."

"Now might not be the time," Mom said.

"No! 'Tis perfect," I said. If I didn't hear what Steigan had to tell me now, I'm not sure I ever would. "Please, go on."

"Here in Dubinshire, I have gathered several domini families together over the cycles for the soul purpose of keeping the memory of Saint Steigan alive. After what I've seen happening in New Lilinar with their domini, I need to make sure the domini don't forget their magical heritage, for magic will return one day and we must be prepared. I've called this group the Onim."

"You want me to record the history of the Onim, don't you?"

"At first, yes, that had been my intention. But I have come to realize that 'tis too dangerous of a task. I can't put you in that position."

"I agree," Ral said.

I pushed back on the bed, trying to sit up further. My abdomen painfully protested but I did it anyway. "Why? Why is it dangerous?"

"Tanold is taking a Plenelian bride and there is nothing the Plenelians hate more than magic. They applaud what his sister has done in taking all magic from the world. And he is continuing the purge his father started. It's only a matter of time before the collective forces of New Lilinar and Plenelia attack Dubinshire. They seek to eradicate every remnant of magic they can, people included." Dad looked down at Vinson. "I'm afraid that the Onim might just be a directory of who to kill first. I cannot stop now. I know how important it will be. I no longer want you involved with the Onim, but that doesn't make recording this child's future as it comes to pass any less important."

Fawla was born a little over a cycle later. All three of our children grew up not knowing that their silly and doting grandfather was the notorious St. Steigan, though they all knew they were descended from Dominus Rivic and they had a special mission to protect the Goddess as Rivic had once done. Steigan took to riding the unicorns on the mountain trails with his grandchildren and taught them how to gather strickleberries, of course. He trained Vinson with a sword, still believing that girls should never have to fight. Steigan also taught him the meaning of the torch-shaped birthmark, a symbol they both should have borne on their palms, but only Steigan had.

During this time, Steigan cautiously grew the Onim. He had penned enough books to hand out to the domini remaining faithful to his cause. Even Ral bowed before Steigan and swore fidelity. It was just the kind of thing Steigan hated, which was why Ral had done it, but I loved the sight and my heart sang, even though I also now knew the danger involved. As more friends came into our lives, each with their own families, I felt it strange how quickly the sins of the past were covered over by celebrations of the present. It was a good thing.

One afternoon, Ral came into the Temple library and leaned close to me. "Where's your father?"

"I haven't seen him all day. Not even at morning service." When I realized that, an edge of panic slid into my stomach. "I'd think he'd be at the house. Is something wrong?"

Ral slid into a chair and gave a furtive glance around as though making sure he wasn't being overheard. "I'm not sure. Word has come in that soldiers are wanted in New Lilinar. Some of the Onim are thinking about going. It might be a way to infiltrate their Temple."

"Why would they want this?" I asked, wondering what information I had missed. "You sound like we're on the brink of war with both sides acting like kindling waiting for the spark."

"My literary wife," he said, touching my cheek. "I want your father's opinion on what he thinks they're up to. He is so certain they are going to attack Dubinshire. 'Tis like he knows something we don't. I mean, 'tis happening just like your father said it would. They aren't going to let magic or the memory of it exist anywhere. We've got to support the true domini remaining in New Lilinar before they are turned against us."

"You wouldn't be one of the ones who was thinking of going, would you?"

"Our world needs for St. Steigan's legacy to live on. The Onim needs to walk in the strength of his shadow and we must do what needs to be done." Hearing Ral speak with such conviction scared me. I knew he loved being a dominus, but to realize he was ready to lay down his life for a small group of domini believing in something that could at any second be considered treason was a terrifying thought.

"Why?" I grabbed his arm, wishing I could make him see reason. "Why is this so vitally important? The word of the Goddess is in our hearts."

"Because our eyes are closer to our brain. A heart cannot see for itself but is fed emotional images sent from our brain.

If the wrong messages get sent, our heart believes the wrong thing."

"But this undertaking is so dangerous," I said, turning toward him. I needed him to understand my fear. "What is the Onim protecting?"

"Dubinshire currently holds the true religion and history, not New Lilinar with their changed texts. New Lilinar seeks to become the civilization of power in our world. Our own Temple has the potential for the same weaknesses that created the false religion in New Lilinar and your father fears that corruption most of all. If Dubinshire fell..."

"Everything would be lost," I finished for him. "If magic returned..."

"It will. Your father says Keteria's spell is only temporary."

"...and Dubinshire no longer had texts from this time or Alityka's, all would be lost. Do you really believe Dubinshire could fall?"

"We have high mountainous terrain; New Lilinar has flat lands for growing crops and raising animals. We don't have the resources to hold out in a long siege. New Lilinar will win eventually. The Onim must protect the true word and preserve the rites as they've been passed through the ages. We might be the only hope for that day when magic returns."

I remembered looking at many of the books Steigan had spent his life writing and remembered how I couldn't read them. Could Ral? "It doesn't sound like either place is safe. Are you sure we should have our family right where war could break out at any moment?"

"You and our son are descendants of Rivic. You yourself are from Lilinar. Like it or not, 'tis in your blood. Rivic's cause is still just and right. We need to fight for your homeland and everything that Rivic believed in. Until New Lilinar comes to their senses, we have to side with Dubinshire."

As Ral stared at me with his dark green eyes, I realized I

was standing on a precipice and he was asking me to make the leap, to decide what I believed. Did I hold true to my faith, my family, my values, my powerful birthright, or did I cast all that history aside for a future void of magic and hope? I knew what side Ral had taken. Could I join him? Did I have the strength he had, or that of Dominari Steigan? My own mother had lost so much when magic had been taken from the world, yet she'd still had to forge on with her life. Did I even have her strength? I had been born in the time of magic but I'd never known it like my mother had, or like Steigan had. But if I was to believe what I'd been hearing my father say, someday magic would return and the people had to be prepared for it. I had to choose: did I support the legends or did I turn my back from the history that had been so close it had nearly destroyed me?

I wasn't sure I could make the jump. While I'd had years of emotional healing, the lies still held hurtful shadows over me. Would I linger here or would I walk into the same light Ral did?

Ral shifted and I felt something I couldn't identify withdraw from me. It was like I still had his love, but he no longer approved of me. I had to choose.

"The Temple has many historians," I said. "I want to be the Onim historian. Who will tell their story? Certainly not you domini."

Ral's eyes lit up and I knew I'd won him back. I don't know if he'd felt it as strongly as I did, but I didn't really care. In fact, it didn't really matter. I'd made my own decision and I'd just been changed. What Ral had taken from me and returned had been the magic of the bond between us and if real magic was anything as powerful, I knew now why my mother had mourned its loss so.

"I knew you'd understand," he said, covering my hand with his. "Your father's message is strong, strong enough to weave through you unseen. I must go. I still seek your father's council."

He stood, kissed the top of my head, and made to leave.

I grabbed onto his hand as I replayed our conversation in my head. What had he meant in saying that Steigan's message had reached me unseen? Was I now a pawn in this mission? Did St. Steigan really care about anyone or anything other than completing his mission? I remembered the words he'd said the day I found out he was taking my mother in marriage, that he didn't want me to see him as a monster, and I knew I had to go now to tell him of my decision and that I'd done it on my own. He may have set me on this path, but it was my decision to walk it alongside Ral.

"Wait, please? I'll go with you." I shuffled my papers together, closed my books, and gathered my belongings as quick as I could. After I packed, Ral took my bag and hoisted it onto his shoulder.

Sapere Hyrin stopped us at the door. "Have you seen Dominus Searn?" he asked me.

Unbelievable! Why did everyone assume I knew where he was at all times? I couldn't help but to smile. If everyone thought we were that close, it was a testament to our family bond. "I was just on my way to find him."

"Can you give him a message for me?"Hyrin asked, handing a sealed envelope toward Ral.

Ral took the letter with a nod. "Whatever you need, Sapere."

Ral and I hurried to my parents' house. I touched Ral's arm as we arrived to get his attention. "Ma probably has the kids with her out in the garden. You go get them; they love it when you arrive first. I'll tell Da you're here."

I went into the house and found Dad in his library, working away at his desk. He noticed me in the doorway and looked up. The familiar look of sadness glistened in his eyes, yet seemed heavier now as if he knew something but couldn't bring forth the bad news. Then he smiled. No matter what, that grin always said that everything was going to be okay.

Why then, didn't it press away the despair in the room? Something was different this time.

I approached the desk to see what he'd been doing. "Da, Ral is here and he has a letter from Sapere Hyrin." I looked at the books he had before him. One, his personal journal, was open to a page he'd folded and sewn into the binding. I recognized the picture. It was one I'd drawn for him many cycles ago showing us together on the day after the Springsday Festival when families went out to gather strickleberries. Hidden among the trees was a unicorn, watching us. I tried to think back to that moment: had I actually seen it there? I hadn't known of his connection to the unicorns back then.

His hand covered mine. "Thank you. I'm nearly done here. Tell him I'll be along shortly."

I noticed three books I hadn't seen before on the table. The covers looked new as if he'd just finished them. Beautiful scrolling writing seemed to link them all together as if the covers had been inked as a single page. I started to reach for them, my heart accelerating even as my breath caught in my throat. I wanted to touch the books, open them and look at the words within, but I didn't feel it was right. I looked at Dad. "It's magnificent." I couldn't stop myself from opening the cover.

Dad brushed his fingers over the page. Golden sparks spun around the scrolling letters in his wake and sparkled off the parchment into the air.

"I wish you'd shown this to me as a little girl," I said, coming around behind him and placing my hand on his shoulder. I looked at the page again, hoping that having it in the proper perspective would make it so I could read the words, and found myself disappointed.

"I couldn't have you playing with them," he said. "These will someday be the most important texts in the world and I can't have pages missing."

I touched the journal. "You put my drawings in that one?"

All of them," he said with a chuckle, "Even the awful portrait of me."

"Awful! Ma says it's a damn good likeness."

Dad got silent and I felt the slight slump in his shoulders as heavy thoughts came to him. I wished to ask what they were, but I think I feared what words would come as much as he did. I squeezed his shoulder hoping that he realized I was marking the moment as everything being good between us before I left. Before I closed the door behind me, I looked back to see him pick up his quill once more.

Mom and Ral sat at the table as I entered the kitchen. Mom put her fingers to her lips and said in a hushed tone, "The children have been napping. We'll let them sleep a little longer."

"I hope you haven't let them sleep too long, Ma," I said to her as Dad emerged from his library. "They come over here and you let them take a long afternoon nap. Then we go home and they run me ragged all night after they've gotten a good sleep."

"Sleep," Dad said, almost a mutter to himself.

Ral handed the letter to him. "Sapere Hyrin asked me to give this to you," Ral said, but I'm not sure Dad was listening.

Deep in thought, Dad turned toward the hallway and pointed in the general direction of the children. "They are peaceful when they're sleeping. They could be moved. We moved them before and they stayed asleep."

"Da?" I asked.

He tapped his index finger against his lips for a moment.

"Thanks to you, I have figured this out. You have just saved the world. It was so simple." He stepped across the room to me and gave me a big hug.

"What are you talking about? How?"

He tore open the letter and read it as he joined us at the table. Then he looked to Ral. "It's time."

I looked at the parchment still partially folded on the table. "Time for what?" I asked, still hoping for real answers. I seized the letter and turned it to look at the single line written on it: The centaurs are moving along Ispion Creek.

Why did it always seem to be riddles with Steigan?

"I'm going to borrow Ral for a fortnight," Dad answered.

The thought of Ral being away for so many nights.... "Why? Please, Dad, give me some answers this time." I glanced at Mom. Her gaze was lowered to the table. I hadn't seen her looking away from Steigan like that in a long time. Something was passing between the three of them. They knew. I had only this moment to prove myself to them. "I want to be historian for the Onim. It's my decision and I've made it. But don't tell me to walk the line with hearsay like you did with Hyrin. If you want me to hold the truth for the Onim, then I need answers."

Everyone looked to me as if I'd doused the forge with a bucket of water. Was it so much of a shock to them that I wanted to be part of this too?

"When Ral returns, he will tell you all the details," Dad said. "You must record his story and keep track of the lives of the families in the Onim. They need to know their history. They need to remember why they are vital. They can't forget."

So many questions jumped in my head at once. "What if Ral doesn't return?"

He reached over and rubbed my shoulder. "Ral will return. His trip isn't dangerous. And I need you to record the events as you have come to learn them from me and your studies. Keep the legend of St. Steigan in the Onim's heart. Its faith in St. Steigan will protect the ones who are trying to save the world. Everything is connected and nothing happens without reason."

"What are you doing on this trip? Are you going to meet with the centaurs? Is Ral going off to do something different than you?"

"Let me show you something important." Steigan held his hand out in front of him. "Cazidor." A small fire lit in his palm.

I jumped back in my chair and I heard Ral inhale a deep breath.

"Magic is a natural force in the world. It's been taken from us for now," Steigan explained. "I'm the only one with power left. Those in the Temple of New Lilinar must know this and learn to fear my power. Saint Steigan will rise again and they must cower." He closed his fingers over his palm, extinguishing the small fire.

"You're returning to New Lilinar?"

"I am."

"You don't expect to come back."

Mom got up from the table. "I think... I hear the children calling." She vanished deeper into the house.

"Ral, take your wife home. We will leave as planned... in the morning."

I looked to Ral, who was staring hard at Steigan. They had already talked about this! Ral nodded, then assisted me to my feet.

I rushed forward and hugged Steigan. "I don't want you to leave."

Steigan squeezed his hug harder than I've ever felt. "I love you, Annae, my daughter."

Sea, Vinson, and Fawla didn't look like they'd been awake

long when we went to gather them. Every step I took away from my parents' house felt heavier than the last. Before we were home, I started to cry. "Stop him, please, Ral. Make sure he comes back to us."

"Go out to the gardens," Ral said as we reached our home. "I'll bring some food out. You need some fresh air."

I followed Fawla outside, half numb, when her squeal of delight scared me back to myself. "Mama, look!" She pointed at a new bush that had been planted there.

A little strickleberry bush had been planted in the garden and a folded note twisted in the light evening breeze from one of its thorny branches. I carefully removed the note and read it.

Strickleberries are a sign of fortune and prosperity. Watching you grow has brought me an abundance I never thought I'd be blessed with. I thank the Goddess for each day I had with you. Your mother has a bush of her own now too. Please tell her the same, for I cherished her friendship and her forgiveness always. Love, Steigan.

I screamed. Ral rushed out, his sword drawn. I flung myself at Ral, who dropped his sword at my onslaught. "He's leaving forever, isn't he? He's not going to live through this."

Nothing more was said and Ral left the next morning before I woke. He returned a fortnight later as he promised, but his thoughts and mood remained distant.

A month later, Ral gathered the Onim together for Sapere Hyrin to deliver the news. "Word has come today that St. Steigan once again walked through the Temple in New Lilinar," Hyrin said. "He vowed he'd rise again when the time came and that as long as he existed, magic would too. Then he disappeared, right before the eyes of every sapere at morning service. 'Tis said that Holy Sapere Tanold fled for Plenelia after that and that New Lilinar is now without a leader. I worry Sapere Olierex will claim power, though he fears Saint Steigan as well. For now, New Lilinar won't be attacking and Dubinshire is safe. Dominari Steigan has bought us more time."

Ral glanced at me. "Here, here! May he find happiness in the afterlife with his Queen Keteria until that day when he returns." Ral raised his mug in toast and after everyone drank, he continued, "We must be prepared for the long road ahead of us. Keep your word strong and teach your children well. The Onim now picks up his mantel and we must carry through with his plan."

Families in the Onim disbursed, moving further into hiding, meeting in secret but never forgetting.

My mother lived for several more cycles. Steigan had left her a comfortable life and she never had to worry for anything. But every now and then, I'd find her looking down the lane as though expecting him to be walking toward her. I think she always maintained that hope.

After her death, I burned the Memory Plaque containing my step-brother's hair with our mother's body during her Crossing Blessing. The fire darkened and splintered the glass, but the iron work remained intact. My own husband cleaned up the metal and had new glass put into it with hair from our children pressed between it. The plaque now hangs in our bedroom. For all the work Steigan did for other people, this is his only piece that I possess. I'm glad to have it. I wish I could tell him how much it means to me.

I had nothing left in Dubinshire. Ral and I moved to a new town settling called Whalston. From here, it was only a three day ride to New Lilinar. Several other Onim families relocated there with us.

With the help of Steigan's long-time friend, Jaxsen Setherbern, I secured a position as an assistant historian for the Temple in New Lilinar. It's one thing to hear that something has happened, but another to see the devastation. I held the palimpsests created from Steigan's pilfered words and learned of the circumstance behind them. I knew now why he sometimes seemed to have memorized his lessons incorrectly. In Dubinshire, he'd been able to save the true word of the Goddess. Saint and traitor were nothing but New Lilinar's pretty little words for scapegoat.

Every now and again, I'd go in and kneel down by the scorch marks on the floor of the Temple's main hall. Many were faded, but one was darker, more recent. Somewhere, among the waning reminders of The Breaking, my father had fallen and given his life to save Dominari Steigan. The freshly blackened area was said to be the spot where St. Steigan had vanished. Even my tears couldn't wash it away.

St. Steigan was many things: a powerful maege, an undefeated dominus, thief, conspirator, traitor, and killer. But what they don't mention is that he was also a champion. Champions sometimes have to make hard decisions. His decision was to finish his mission.

We, the Onim, must be ready for St. Steigan's return.

READY FOR ANOTHER QUEST?

Sign up for Dawn Blair's newsletter to learn about new releases, get access to fun and free stuff, hear about events, and more!

It's easy.

Go to **www.morningskystudios.net/newsletter** to join the adventure.

The prophecy has been fulfilled: the Bloody Saint has returned.

Now his enemies attack the gates of the ruined city of Lilinar to capture him. There will be no escape for him this time and no saving his friends. He has nothing but the debris around him.

And the advantage of a lifetime to plan.

THE ADVENTURE CONTINUES

www.morningskystudios.net

Follow the series at
dawnblair.wordpress.com

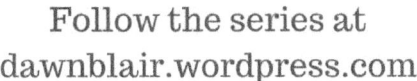

About the Author

Dawn Blair grew up on a ranch in a rural Nevada town. The old buildings provided inspiration for her imagination as she thrived on stories of unicorns, princesses, heroic knights, and hidden doors to other dimensions.

For as long as she can remember, Dawn has had a passion for storytelling. Though she started out writing, her creative life expanded into painting and illustration.

She loves creating worlds and spinning tales for people to enjoy. The best ones are the stories that surprise her as she's writing. She loves her characters doing the unexpected. She'll gladly tell you that the most exciting part about being a writer is being the first one on the journey.

Thank you for taking the time to join her on these adventures.

Find more about Dawn and read free fiction on her blog at:
dawnblair.wordpress.com

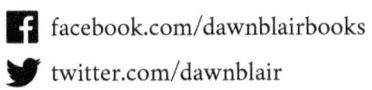

facebook.com/dawnblairbooks

twitter.com/dawnblair